3

Mrs Hobbs lived next door. "There's a dog woofing in your house," she said to Jess, as the family arrived at home. "Please tell me you haven't got a dog?"

Jess smiled. "No, we definitely haven't got a dog, Mrs Hobbs," she promised.

"What a relief!" said Mrs Hobbs. "We don't like dogs, do we, George?" she said, stroking her fluffy white cat.

Waffle
The Wonder Dog

Scholastic Children's Books,
Euston House, 24 Eversholt Street,
London NW1 1DB, UK

A division of Scholastic Ltd
London ~ New York ~ Toronto ~ Sydney ~ Auckland
Mexico City ~ New Delhi ~ Hong Kong

Published in the UK by Scholastic Ltd, 2019
Waffle The Wonder Dog © and TM Darrall Macqueen Ltd 2019
Written by Emily Stead © Scholastic Children's Books

TRADE EDITION ISBN 978 1407 19829 3
SCHOLASTIC CLUBS AND FAIRS EDITION ISBN 978 1407 19937 5

Printed and bound in Italy by L.E.G.O S.p.A

2 4 6 8 10 9 7 5 3 1

FSC
www.fsc.org
MIX
Paper from
responsible sources
FSC® C023419

www.scholastic.co.uk

5430000509592 1

It was the day of the Brooklyn-Bells' wedding. Evie's mum, Jess, had just got married to Doug's dad, Simon. They were all going to be living together as one family for the first time. It was also the day that the Brooklyn-Bells met Waffle.

Inside, the house was all ready for the wedding party.

"Can we open some of the wedding presents?" Evie asked.

"In a minute!" said Jess.

Just then, Evie heard a noise. *Woof! Woof!* it went. Then she saw something very strange. A pink box was moving all by itself. Evie followed it. When it stopped moving, she carefully lifted up the box.

"A puppy!" Evie gasped.

The puppy looked up at Evie. Then it ran through the cat flap, out into the garden.

"Puppy, come back!" said Evie. "My name is Evie."

Evie fetched a sausage from the party food for the puppy, who gobbled up the tasty treat. *Yum! Yum!*

Then the puppy scampered off to hide under the table.

"Hey!" said Doug crossly. "Evie has opened the wedding presents without us."

Simon picked up one of the presents. "This box is all wet and sticky," he said. "Evie, are these your teeth marks?"

"No!" laughed Evie. "A puppy opened the presents, come and see!"

Doug, Simon and Jess followed Evie to the table. But when she lifted up the tablecloth, the puppy had disappeared!

"He was under there, I promise," said Evie sadly. She went to look for the puppy in the garden, but he was nowhere to be seen.

A couple of minutes later, Doug tapped on the bedroom window. "I've found him!" he called down to Evie.

Evie dashed into the house and up to the bedroom.

"This is who opened the presents!" Evie explained.

"What's my dad going to say?" asked Doug.

"What's my mum going to say?" asked Evie.

"Say about what?" asked Jess, appearing at the door.

"Nothing!" said Evie and Doug together, hiding the puppy.

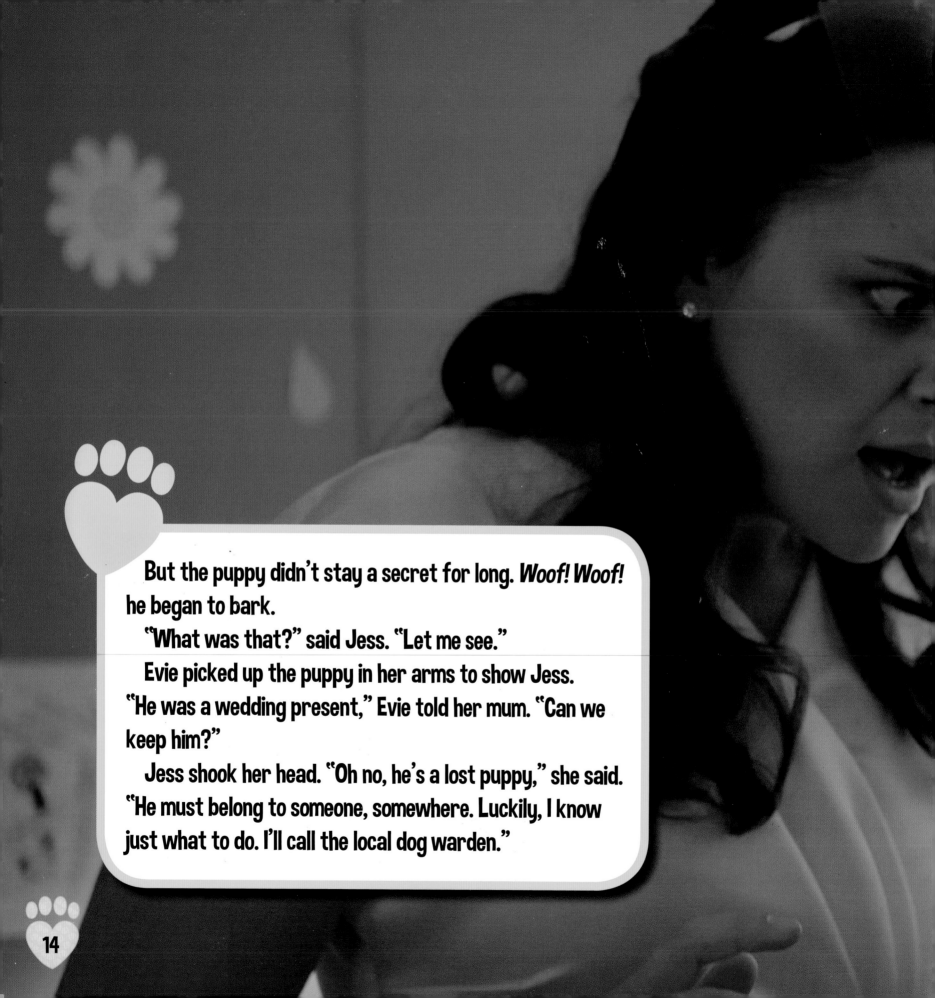

But the puppy didn't stay a secret for long. *Woof! Woof!* he began to bark.

"What was that?" said Jess. "Let me see."

Evie picked up the puppy in her arms to show Jess. "He was a wedding present," Evie told her mum. "Can we keep him?"

Jess shook her head. "Oh no, he's a lost puppy," she said. "He must belong to someone, somewhere. Luckily, I know just what to do. I'll call the local dog warden."

Ding! Dong! The doorbell rang. The puppy scampered out of the bedroom.

"I thought we said no dogs?" said Simon, surprised. He picked up the puppy to give him a cuddle. "Even cute ones that lick and tickle!"

Downstairs, Evie's grandpa let himself into the house. Gramps loved dogs!

"We've got a puppy," said Evie, hurrying down the stairs. "Come and see!"

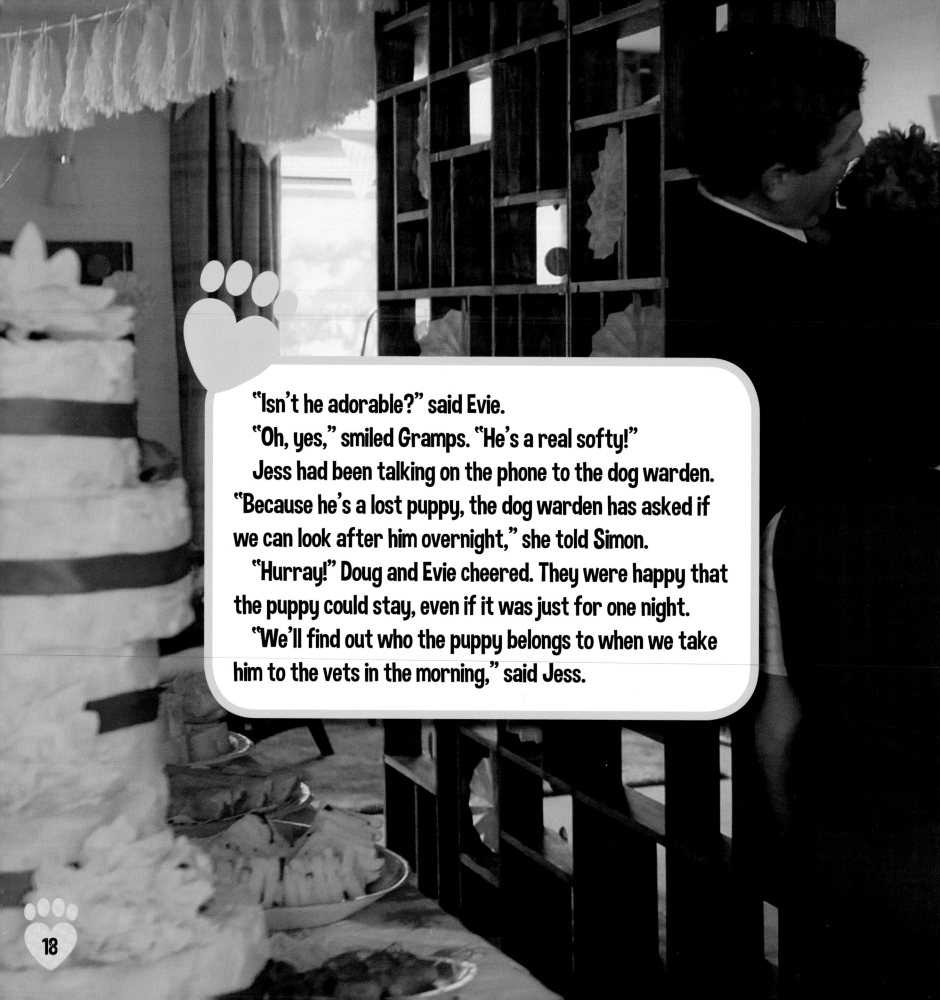

"Isn't he adorable?" said Evie.

"Oh, yes," smiled Gramps. "He's a real softy!"

Jess had been talking on the phone to the dog warden. "Because he's a lost puppy, the dog warden has asked if we can look after him overnight," she told Simon.

"Hurray!" Doug and Evie cheered. They were happy that the puppy could stay, even if it was just for one night.

"We'll find out who the puppy belongs to when we take him to the vets in the morning," said Jess.

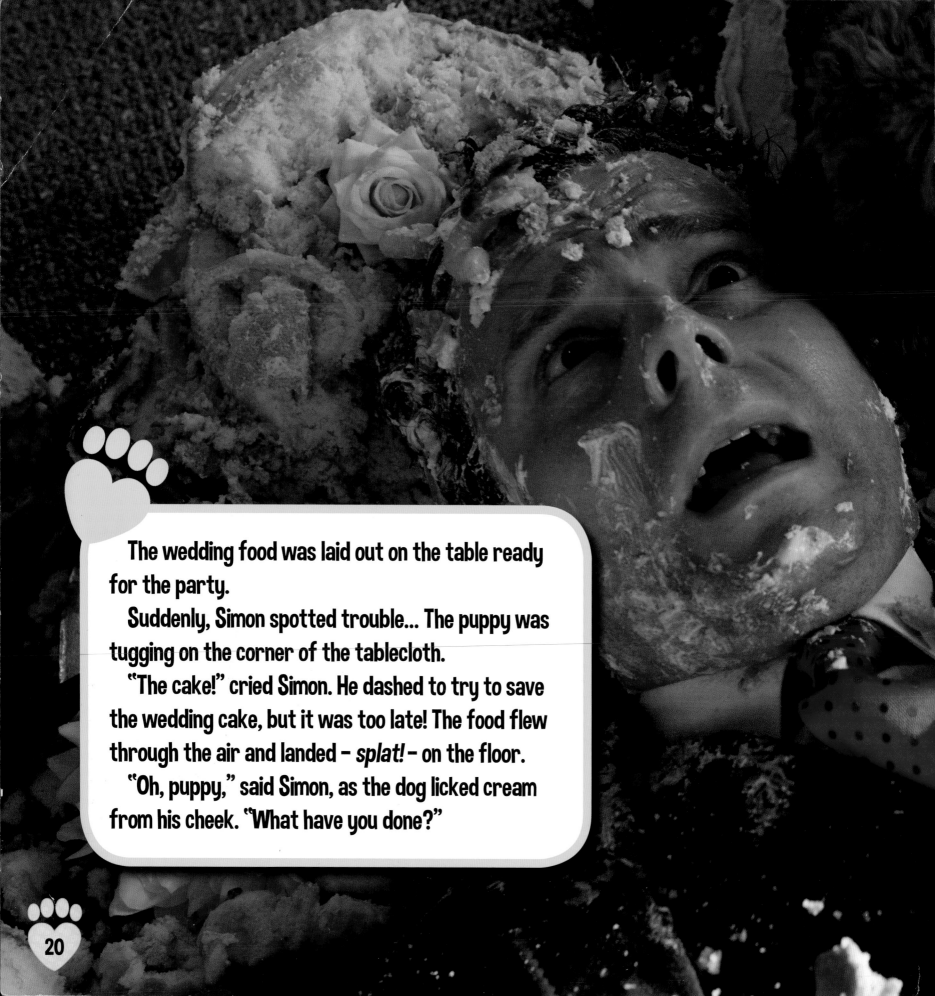

The wedding food was laid out on the table ready for the party.

Suddenly, Simon spotted trouble... The puppy was tugging on the corner of the tablecloth.

"The cake!" cried Simon. He dashed to try to save the wedding cake, but it was too late! The food flew through the air and landed – *splat!* – on the floor.

"Oh, puppy," said Simon, as the dog licked cream from his cheek. "What have you done?"

There was just enough time to tidy up before the guests arrived for the party.

Everyone enjoyed themselves. And they all loved the puppy!

"What a wedding day!" smiled Simon, when all the guests had gone home.

"And we had an extra surprise guest!" laughed Doug.

In the kitchen, Evie and the puppy were snuggling under the table. If he was staying, Evie would have to give him a name, she thought.

"Woof ... Woofy ... Woofle?" Evie suggested. But none of those names sounded quite right. "How about Waffle?" she said.

Woof! barked the puppy, wagging his tail.

Evie smiled. "Do you like the name Waffle?"

"Yes," said the puppy. "Thank you!"

Evie could not believe her ears – Waffle could talk! Waffle was a Wonder Dog! And their amazing adventures were about to begin.